WILLOW VALLEY

Spooky Sleepover

Tracey Corderoy

Illustrated by Hannah Whitty

First published in the UK in 2012 by Scholastic Children's Books
An imprint of Scholastic Ltd
Euston House, 24 Eversholt Street
London, NW1 1DB, UK
Registered office: Westfield Road, Southam, Warwickshire, CV47 0RA
SCHOLASTIC and associated logos are trademarks and/
or registered trademarks of Scholastic Inc.

Text copyright © Tracey Corderoy, 2012
Illustration copyright © Hannah Whitty, 2012

The rights of Tracey Corderoy and Hannah Whitty to be identified as the
author and illustrator of this work have been asserted by them.

Cover illustration © Hannah Whitty, 2012

ISBN 978 1 407 12475 9

A CIP catalogue record for this book
is available from the British Library

Printed and bound by CPI Group (UK) Ltd, Croydon, CR0 4YY
Papers used by Scholastic Children's Books
are made from wood grown in sustainable forests.

1 3 5 7 9 10 8 6 4 2

This is a work of fiction. Names, characters, places, incidents
and dialogues are products of the author's imagination or are used
fictitiously. Any resemblance to actual people, living or dead,
events or locales is entirely coincidental.

www.scholastic.co.uk/zone
www.traceycorderoy.com

For Anna, with all my love. . .

T.C xx

WILLOW VALLEY

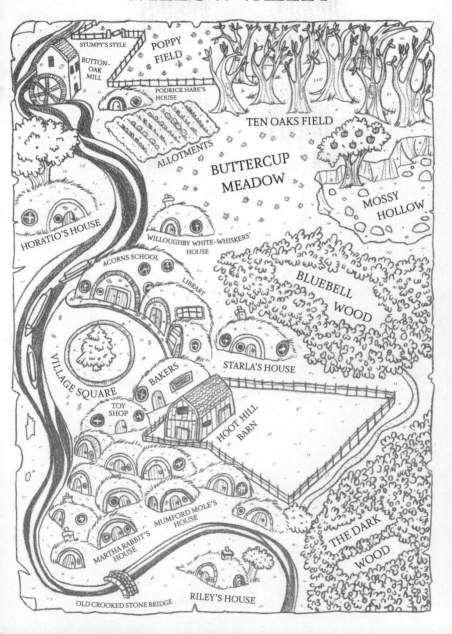

Chapter 1

It was late afternoon and a big golden sun beamed down on Riley's garden. Fat bumblebees wriggled into the foxgloves standing by the old shed and the soft green grass was dotted with little daisies.

Riley was sitting on his garden wall peering down the hill at the whole of Willow Valley. His two best friends should be arriving any minute.

He swung his legs as he waited,

watching an ant dragging a very large
leaf behind him!

Suddenly, Riley's ears pricked up
and a smile spread from whisker to
whisker. And *then* he spotted them –

two fluffy dots down at the bottom of the hill. His friends, Horatio and Starla, were nearly here.

"Yippee!" cried Riley, leaping off the wall and racing down the hill through the long, swishy grass to meet them. They were all camping out in his garden that night. Riley couldn't wait! He'd never, *ever* camped out before. It was going to be brilliant!

Horatio Spark, a roly-poly hedgehog, was pulling a trolley piled with food behind him. His chubby checks were the colour of two bright cherries.

"Phew!" he panted as Riley appeared.

"I *think* I've remembered everything."
He puffed out his chest and proudly
nodded at his trolley.

"See?" beamed Horatio. "For our
midnight feast! Ginger biscuits . . . ginger
cake . . . and three gingerbread men, which
I made with these *very* paws this morning!"

Horatio loved nothing more than a
little snack or two – unless you counted
tightrope walking or rolling down hills
super-fast, or trying (as he did most
evenings) to catapult himself to the moon!

"Oh *no*!" cried Horatio suddenly,
peering further into the trolley. "I've
forgotten my pyjamas! Oh well, never

mind – at least I remembered all the important stuff!"

"What have you brought, Starla?" asked Riley, feeling sure she wouldn't have forgotten anything. Starla was the cleverest badger he knew, after Willoughby White-Whiskers, her grandfather

Willoughby was the captain of Willow Valley's fleet of narrowboats, which the animals used to go on market trips down the river, to sell their goods. Willoughby White-Whiskers was also Riley's hero.

"Well, I remembered my pyjamas," smiled Starla. "And I've brought a spare nightie just in case, and my hairbrush, toothbrush and a fairy-tale book. Oh, and I've got something for you and Horatio too!"

She opened a pocket on the side of her rucksack and pulled out three small torches.

"*Wow*," gasped Horatio.

"Thanks!" cried Riley. "But where did you get them?"

Starla smiled as she handed the red torch to Riley and the blue one to Horatio. "Grandpa Willoughby gave them to me when I said we were camping in your garden. He told me about the first time he camped out and said these would be very useful."

Starla slipped her purple torch back into her rucksack for safekeeping. "I've brought some snap cards too," she said.

"Great!" cried Riley, and he walked back up the hill beside them until they reached his garden.

"Right," he said, leading them in, "the first job that we need to do is put up the tent. I had a go earlier but didn't . . . um, get very far. . ."

He pointed at a muddle of tent bits lying in the long grass. "Where are the instructions?" Starla asked.

"They're here somewhere," Riley said, thrusting a paw into the mountain of poles and pegs and pulling out a sheet of instructions.

"We don't need *instructions!*" cried Horatio, whisking the sheet from Riley's paws before he could pass it to Starla.

"But how *else* will we know how to put up the tent?" said Starla.

"Bah!" cried Horatio. "I know how to do it! Putting up a tent is as easy as pie! I wish it *was* pie, though. I'm starving!"

Grinning, he folded the instruction sheet into a paper aeroplane.
"Instructions are *useless!*" Horatio cried.

"But *aeroplanes* . . . now we're talking!"

"Horatio – no – don't *throw* it!" gasped Riley. But it was too late. Horatio already had.

"Wheee!" he chuckled as a sudden breeze blew it up – up – up and away! Riley and Starla watched, wide-eyed.

"It's quite some flyer!" Riley nodded.

"Yes," agreed Starla, "but that doesn't help us put up our tent."

"But I *told* you!" beamed Horatio. "Leave it to me!"

He bounded over to the pile of tent bits as Starla and Riley flumped on to some toadstools.

"Oh dear," sighed Starla, shaking her head as they watched. . .

"Tum-te-tum!" Horatio hummed to himself as he balanced tent poles on his nose, then played games of darts with the pegs.

Clearly, he didn't have a *clue* how a tent went up. Nor did he seem to care very much either!

When he threw the tent around his shoulders and pretended to be *"Superhog!"* Starla and Riley finally decided to lend a helping paw.

They hurried over, whisked off his cape, and then all three of them worked out how to put up the tent together.

By the time they'd finished, the garden felt cooler and the mossy smell of evening filled the air. Riley gazed up at their wonky tent. It would do just fine! Very soon it would be getting dark and

they'd be huddled inside it together.
Butterflies danced in Riley's tummy at
the thought!

"Oh *wait*!" cried Starla, frowning at
Horatio. "What is that pole in your paw?"

"Um!" said Horatio, his ears turning pink. "Err, this is . . . a *spare* tent pole, of course! Tents *always* have spare poles, you know."

"Err. . ." muttered Riley, "I don't think they do."

"Do you think we should start again?" asked Starla.

"No way!" cried Horatio. "It's supper time – look – *there*!"

He pointed a prickly paw down the garden. Riley's mum and sister were coming along the path, carrying marshmallows speared on long, thin twigs and a plateful of fat pink sausages.

"Riley!" squealed Mimi-Rose, waving a stick. "We're all having supper in the garden! Mum's going to light an *enormous* campfire and cook the marshmallows and all these sausages! *And*," she whispered as they got a bit closer, "I might camp out too!"

"I've told you already, Mimi-Rose," said their mum, "you're too small to camp out. But I've got you all a *delicious* supper!"

"Hooray!" cried Riley. "Let's collect sticks! We need lots and lots for the campfire!"

"Nice dry ones," called his mum as they darted everywhere.

"OK!" squeaked Riley excitedly.

When the sticks had been gathered, Riley's mum carefully lit the campfire and cooked all the sausages. Then they huddled around the dancing flames, nibbling sausages and toasting marshmallows and singing funny campfire songs.

For pudding, they all had raspberry
ice cream, which they ate as the sky
turned pink. Then moths began to flutter
around the trees and stars twinkled
down from the sky as they watched the
flames of their campfire grow smaller
and smaller.

When it was finally out, Riley's mum took Mimi-Rose back inside and Riley and his friends crawled into their lopsided tent, ready for their camp-out to begin.

Chapter 2

It felt all cosy inside the tent as the friends laid out their sleeping bags and pillows. Then Riley and Starla changed into their pyjamas.

"What shall we do now?" Riley asked, rubbing his little paws together. "It's *way* too early to go to sleep!"

"Let's play games!" Horatio cried.

"How about snap?" said Starla.

"Hooray!" cheered Riley. Everyone loved snap.

Starla found her cards and dealt them out. Then the game of snap began. It was tricky playing snap with Horatio though, because every time someone put down a card, he'd wallop the pile with a prickly paw, shouting, "Snap! Snap! Snap!" even if the cards didn't match.

"That's cheating, Horatio!" Riley frowned.

"It isn't!" grinned Horatio. "There's nothing in the rules that says you can't snap when you want to."

They carried on. . .

"Snap!" cried Horatio.

"Snap!"

"Snap!"

"SNAP!" In no time at all, he had won *all* the cards. "I'm the best at snap in the whole of Willow Valley! Maybe the world!" he cried.

"Only because of your prickly paws!" laughed Starla.

Riley shook his head. "I need the toilet. When I come back, let's play something else."

With that, he pattered off to the toilet as the others packed up the cards. When he returned, he was shivery cold. "Brrr!" he said. "It's chilly out there and it's getting *really* dark! Did you decide what we should play next?"

Horatio and Starla smiled at each other. "Pillow fight time!" they cried. They snatched up their pillows and started whacking Riley from each side. He squealed with delight, then grabbed his own pillow too.

"Ha!" he giggled, as Starla's pillow burst open on Horatio's prickly head.

"Hee hee!" laughed Horatio. "Hey, everyone – watch *this*!"

He tossed his pillow into the air and headed it like a football. It split open at once and feathers rained down like fluffy snowflakes.

"Uh-oh," said Riley, now knee-deep in feathers. "Maybe we should stop."

"OK," said Horatio, flopping down on his sleeping bag. "That was fun, though! I really do like camping very much!"

Starla put her own pillow back on her sleeping bag, then got out her fairy-tale book.

"Shall I read us a story now?" she asked.

"Oh yes!" Riley nodded.

"Wait!" cried Horatio. "Not one about fairies . . . or princesses . . . or soppy mermaids!"

"OK," giggled Starla. "I'll choose something else."

She opened her book. "Oh!" she said. "How about Red Riding Hood and the wolf that gobbles up Grandma?"

"Yeah, that's a really good one!" cried Horatio.

Starla found the page. "Oh wait!" she said. "We could *act* out the story instead! I'll be Red Riding Hood. . ."

"And I'll be the wolf!" said Riley
very quickly.

"So . . . who does that leave?" Horatio
asked, scratching his prickly head.
"Hang on a minute . . . *I'm* not being
Grandma!"

He folded his arms, crossed his legs,
and stuck out his bottom lip in a jolly
big pout! It wasn't until Riley tempted
him with a ginger biscuit or two that
Horatio's scowl slowly disappeared and
he *finally* agreed to be Grandma.

"And you can wear this!" Starla
smiled, finding her spare nightie.
"Grandma does wear a nightgown in

the story, you know."

She tossed the frilly pink nightie to Horatio. "Hmmm," said Horatio thoughtfully, "I would, perhaps, wear this . . . if I wasn't so terribly hungry. Those two ginger biscuits I ate just now were really awfully tiny! Now if, say, I could have some ginger cake too, then I'd *definitely* wear the nightie! Only if the cake was a nice big chunk, mind you."

The others agreed and Riley got him some cake, which Horatio wolfed down quickly. Then he squeezed himself into Starla's nightie. Now everyone was ready!

"Once upon a time. . ." Starla began, marching around wrapped in a cloak made out of her red sleeping bag, ". . .a little girl called Red Riding Hood was on her way to visit her lovely, smiley grandma when—"

"Silly nightie!" Horatio blurted out, scratching himself all over. "Silly, frilly, itchy, horrid thing!"

"*Horatio*," Starla sighed, "just try and be quiet until you're eaten, OK?"

"Yeah!" giggled Riley. "By big old, bad old *me*!"

Starla carried on with the story but Horatio would not be quiet. After every few words that Starla said he'd huff or puff, or wriggle or jiggle, or moan or groan, or sigh. . .

"This nightie's too *tight*!"

"And too pink. . ."

"And too ITCHY!"

"And I can do other characters *way* better than Grandma – just try me!"

When they finally got to the Grandma-eating bit, Horatio leapt to his feet. "*Aha!*" he cried in a growly man-voice. "Fooled you all, haven't I?!"

He snatched up the leftover tent pole and chopped it through the air. "I'm NOT Grandma at all! Oh no! I'm really the *woodcutter* who catches the wolf!"

"No – you're the *grandma*. Stop spoiling it!" said Starla.

"Am *not!*" cried Horatio. "I'm the WOODCUTTER! Chop! Chop! Chop!"

He wriggled out of Starla's nightie and stamped his foot hard. "And I'm going out into my forest, by myself, so *there!*"

And with that, he stomped off out of the tent as the other two watched on. A few moments later, he squelched back in.

"Bother!" said Horatio drippily. "It's raining!"

Chapter 3

Horatio marched over to his sleeping bag and plonked himself back down. "I say we do something else," he frowned. "I can make up better stories than silly Red Riding Hood any day!"

"Hey – good idea!" Riley cried. "Let's make up stories. Spooky ones!" It was getting quite dark in the tent now – just right for telling spooky stories.

"You go first, then," Horatio said. "I'm, err – *thinking*!"

He then sneaked a few biscuits from his trolley and, when no one was looking, crammed them all into his mouth.

"OK," nodded Riley. "I'll go first."

He knelt down on his sleeping bag and Starla got out her torch.

"Uuu – 'ood i'ea!" mumbled Horatio, swallowing down the biscuits. "Spooky stories are *way* more spooky by torchlight!"

They turned on their torches but, as they did, "*Tw-whooooooo!*" went something outside.

"*What's that?*" squeaked Riley.

"Dunno!" cried Horatio, rolling up

into a ball.

"It was just an owl," Starla said.
"That's all."

By now, big raindrops were pattering
on to the tent and the wind had started
to moan. And, for the very first time

that night, Riley began to feel scared.

"Go on then, Riley," Starla said. "Tell us a spooky story!"

"Err," shivered Riley, trying to think of one that wouldn't make *him* too afraid. "Um," he said. "O-OK – I think I've got one. . ."

Riley cleared his throat and Horatio uncurled himself, though they both still looked very jumpy. The wind was blowing the flaps of the tent now.

"Um, once there was a . . . *bunny*," Riley began.

"It's got to be *spooky*," said Starla, "remember?"

"I-it *is*!" stuttered Riley. "I'm just getting going, you'll see! So, um, this bunny was in someone's garden, pulling up carrots when—"

"*W-wait!* Was it *night-time*?" Horatio gasped. "Was the wind m-moaning?"

"*No!*" squeaked Riley. "It was a nice sunny day! Anyway, she counted the carrots in the ground and there were four – no – five. Then she turned around—"

"Don't tell me!" cried Starla. "A big, hairy monster came creeping up and. . . *Snap!*"

She clapped her fluffy paws together

and Riley and Horatio jumped. "Bunny was the monster's morning snack!" said Starla.

"No!" shrieked Riley, all of a quiver. "That didn't happen at all! She just counted the carrots, turned around, and when she turned back . . . one carrot was *gone*. Someone – or some*thing* – had stolen it, just like that!"

"Super-scary!" gulped Horatio, but Starla couldn't stop laughing.

"Is *that* your spooky story?" she giggled. "But that's not spooky at all! Right then," she said, still giggling. "My turn!"

Starla settled herself in front of her friends and shone the torch on her face. "Once upon a time there was a moany old ghost who lived all alone on a narrowboat. . ."

Horatio and Riley budged up close.

"N-not a *bunny*?" stuttered Riley.

"No," said Starla. "It was a ghost and it only came out at *night*."

"At night!" gulped the boys.

"At night," nodded Starla, "when the wind was howling like *whoooooo!*"

"Don't do that!" yelled the boys together.

Starla lowered her voice to a whisper. "Well, one night this ghost was sailing its boat and the chains around its neck were clanking."

"Chains?" gasped Riley.

"Clanking?" gulped Horatio.

"*Wait!*" cried Riley. "What's that noise?

I can hear clanking . . . outside . . .
listen!"

Everyone listened. Riley was right.
Something was clanking up the path!

"*ARRGGHH!*" everybody screamed.

"*HIDE!*"

They all dived into their sleeping
bags as the clanking outside got louder
and louder. "I don't really think I like
camping very much!" squeaked Riley.

Then, suddenly, the clanking stopped –
right outside their tent. The flaps either
side of the doorway went *swissshhhhh*.

"Everyone keep still!" whispered Starla. "Then the something might go away." But the thing outside did not go away. Instead, it called in a very loud voice. . . "Cocoa!"

"*Mum!*" gasped Riley, peeping out of his sleeping bag. The others peeped out too.

"And look!" cried Horatio. "That clanking noise was just big mugs of cocoa! Cocoa is my *very* favourite thing!"

Riley's mum passed in three mugs of steaming cocoa on a little wooden tray. "Are you all OK?" she asked. "Not scared or anything?"

"*Us?*" cried the boys. "We're not
scared!"

"We've been telling spooky stories!"
giggled Starla.

Riley's mum kissed him goodnight,
then left the friends to enjoy their
bedtime drink.

"Wait for it to cool a bit!" she called as she hurried back up the wet garden.

"OK," three little voices called back. "Night night. . ."

For a moment, Riley wished *he* was going in too. Back inside to his warm, squashy bed where the wind didn't moan like out here. Where his mum would read him a story with a happy ending!

Chapter 4

While they waited for their cocoa to cool, Starla asked Horatio if he wanted to borrow her nightie, as it was getting very cold in the tent now.

"It makes me feel like *Grandma*," scowled Horatio.

"It's better than nothing," Riley shrugged. "At least it will keep you warm."

"No, thanks," said Horatio with a prickly frown. "I'd rather be cold."

They crawled into their sleeping bags. "Brrr!" said Horatio. "It's as cold as an icicle in here!"

"*Eeek!*" squeaked Riley. He found his nightcap and put it on. At least his head would be warm. "I'll *never* be able to sleep," he grumbled.

"Me neither!" shivered Horatio. "Hey,

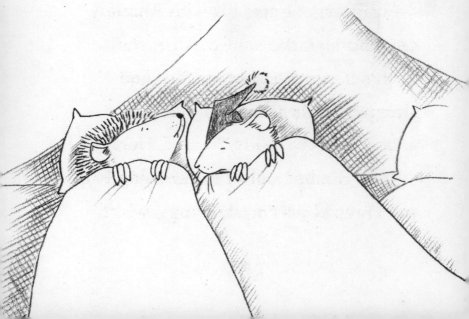

Starla – what's that you've got in your paws?"

Starla carefully unfolded the pink bundle she'd just taken out of her rucksack. "It's my special patchwork blanket!" she replied.

The boys shivered on as she smoothed the blanket down on top of her red sleeping bag. "I made it with Mummy last autumn," she smiled. Then she wriggled into her sleeping bag and plumped up her feathery pillow.

"Is our cocoa ready?" asked Horatio.

Riley climbed out of his sleeping bag and crawled over to the mugs, which

were now only steaming very slightly.
"Oh!" he cried. "I think it is!"

He passed a mug each to Starla and
Horatio and the friends sipped their
cocoa as the wind whipped the tent and
the owl started hooting again.

"I hope he stops nattering soon!"

muttered Riley as he tried, once more, to make himself comfy in a sleeping bag as cold as a fridge! "I'll never be able to sleep with all that din!"

Then, as they were finishing off their drink, Horatio's torch went out. "Oh no," he tutted. What else could go wrong? First, he'd been forced to wear a frilly nightie, then they'd thought they'd heard a ghost, and now his torch had decided not to work! Camping wasn't quite what he'd expected. . .

"*I don't like the dark!*" Horatio wailed. "I think . . . I think . . . I think – *I want to go home!*"

He gave a big, shuddery sniff.

"Oh Horatio," breathed Starla. "Don't be sad!" She wriggled out of her sleeping bag and padded over to him. Great big tears were tumbling from Horatio's eyes.

"Hey," said Riley, patting his arm, "you don't want to go home!"

"Riley's right!" nodded Starla. "We're big, brave campers!"

Horatio gave a sorry squeak. "Well," he said, in a snuffly voice, "I *thought* I was brave . . . b-before I came . . . but now . . . I'm not so sure. . ."

He gave another giant sniff, then stuffed his thumb firmly into his mouth, his little black nose wrinkling up as he sucked it.

Starla nipped to her sleeping bag and came back holding her pillow. "Here," she said, handing it to Horatio. "Why

don't you have this? Look, I even puffed
it up so it's really *fluffy* now!"

"Oh – *Fluffy*!" Riley cried. "I'd
forgotten all about him. Hey, I've got
something for you too, Horatio!"

He pattered over to his rucksack
and pulled out a saggy old teddy.
"Here!" he squeaked. "You can
borrow Fluffy!"

"You've brought *Fluffy*?" Horatio
sniffed. "If I'd have known, I'd have
brought *Bumble* too! I thought that no
one would bring their teddies."

"Of course we would!" Starla smiled.
"I've got Archibald Potts as well – look!"

She stuffed a paw into her sleeping bag and felt around a bit. Then she whisked out a serious-looking honey-coloured bear wearing spectacles and a dark green waistcoat.

"Here!" she said, holding him out. "Borrow Archie too! He always cheers *me* up when I'm sad."

"Oh," breathed Horatio. "Really? I can borrow them *both*?"

Starla and Riley nodded their heads, so Horatio took both teddy bears and snuggled them into his big round tummy. "Thank you," he said, with a little smile.

"No problem!" cried Riley brightly.

"Perhaps we should get some sleep
now?" said Starla. "Would you both like to
share my blanket too? It'll just about fit
over us all if you two move a bit closer."

"Oh thanks, Starla!" cried the boys,
budging up even more.

Starla crawled back into her own
sleeping bag and spread her blanket over

everyone. "Night night, then!" she said.

"Night night!" replied the boys, settling down.

They closed their eyes, but as they did, giant raindrops began drumming on the tent. *Boom – boom – boom!*

"Oh no!" groaned Horatio, sitting back up. "Now there's a storm outside! I'll never get to sleep with those *boom – boom – booms!*"

"Me neither!" moaned Riley, sitting back up too.

Horatio sniffed. "I want to go ho—"

"*Wait!*" cried Starla. "I know what we'll do! How about we have our midnight feast? By the time we've had that, the rain might have stopped!"

"Yay!" cheered Riley. "Midnight feast time!"

"No!" cried Horatio. "I mean," he gulped, "I'm not . . . all that terribly . . . um, hungry."

It went very quiet, except for the rain pounding down on the tent. "You're not *hungry*?" Riley finally squeaked. "But Horatio, you're *always* hungry!"

"*Why* aren't you hungry, Horatio?" asked Starla, turning on her torch. She quickly shone it at Horatio's trolley.

"Oh no," she groaned. "*Horatio.*"

The mountain of food Horatio had brought had all disappeared. There were only a few tiny cakes crumbs left and the head of a gingerbread man.

"Horatio," tutted Starla. "You've eaten the *whole* feast!"

"That was meant to be *shared*!" Riley cried.

Horatio hung his sorry head and heaved a heavy sigh. "I was just a tiny bit frightened," he whispered. "What with horrid hooty owl and the clanking ghost-we-thought-was-a-ghost-but-wasn't-a-ghost-after-all, and the wind that keeps on whooshing about! But I *did* save you both a whole gingerbread head, see?"

He grabbed the little head. "It's *even* got two currant eyes – one for Starla and one for Riley!" Horatio did look very sorry.

"OK," sighed Starla.

"Yeah," muttered Riley. "I'm not all

that hungry anyway. *But,*" he added
quickly, "let's save the head for later, OK?"

Horatio popped it back into the trolley,
and then they got into their sleeping
bags. But, just as they were settling
down *again*. . .

"*Psst!*" whispered Starla. "Riley!
Horatio! There are two eyes peeping in."

"Oh Starla!" said Horatio. "No more
scary stories, please."

"It's not a story, Horatio," squeaked
Riley. "*Look!*"

Chapter 5

The two peeping eyes gave a blink.

Then the creature sneezed, "*Aaa-chooooo!*"

"What *is* it?" whispered Starla,
keeping very, very still.

"A monster!" wailed Horatio.

"No," said Riley, shaking his head.
"It's only tiny!"

As everyone drew a little bit closer,
the eyes at the door grew wide. "It's
OK," whispered Riley to the tiny thing,
"don't be scared."

He turned to Starla. "Hey, pass me a torch and then we can see what it is."

Starla passed him her torch and he shone it at the creature.

"*Awww*," cooed Horatio. "It's kind of cute!"

"Very cute," Starla smiled.

"Poor thing. It must be frightened of the storm," said Riley.

The tiny baby animal sat shivering in the doorway. Its ears lay flat against its soaking fur and its whiskers drooped down, dripping.

It shook its head and a shower of raindrops flew through the air like

shooting stars. But no one could make out
what it was because it was so bedraggled.

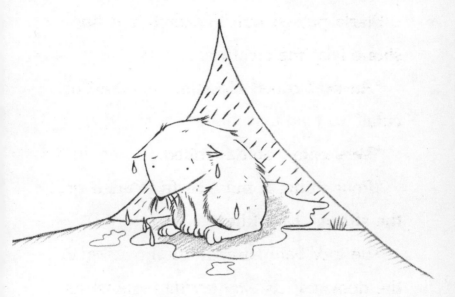

"Is it a bunny?" Riley asked.

"I don't *think* so," whispered Starla.
"Bunnies have fluffy pom-pom tails and
much bigger feet than that."

"It might be a really small hippo?" muttered Horatio.

"Oh dear," said Starla. "It's freezing cold. Hello," she said in a very soft voice, "come to Starla."

The tiny animal blinked again, then slowly padded into the tent. It seemed to prefer Riley though, for it snuggled up close and sniffed him.

"Soggy!" said the little thing suddenly.

"It's a soggy!" Riley cried.

"Oh I *knew* it!" Horatio nodded. "I've read about them before. I think they're a bit like a . . . cow, only different!"

The soggy gave a sudden shiver.

"Here," said Riley, "have this." And
he wrapped the little thing in Starla's
blanket.

"Are you hungry?" Starla asked the
little creature. The soggy didn't answer,
but suddenly his tummy gave a giant
rumble.

"He *is*!" cried Horatio. "Hey, me too! What can we feed him? Let's see. . ."

He found the little gingerbread head and held it out to the soggy. "Here you are," Horatio smiled. "Supper!"

The soggy gave it a tiny sniff . . . then wolfed it down whole. *"Whoa!"* cried Horatio. "I was right. He *was* hungry!"

They looked at the soggy, then at each other. "What shall we do with him now?" asked Riley.

"Maybe he's tired?" Starla said. "If we snuggle him down, he might go to sleep."

"But he must be lost!" Horatio cried. "He must want to find his mummy!"

"We can help him do that tomorrow," said Riley. "I'm not going out in that horrible storm. Anyway, I wouldn't be allowed."

"Yes," nodded Starla. "Riley's right.

We'll help him find his mummy in the morning."

She climbed back into her sleeping bag. Riley and Horatio did the same.

"He'll be safe enough here until morning," said Starla. The others nodded and settled back down, but they could hear quiet sniffling and snuffling. The soggy was crying!

"Oh!" said Starla. "Maybe he wants to be read a bedtime story?"

So the friends took turns to read the soggy stories from Starla's book. The little creature loved *Puss in Boots* and *The Magic Porridge Pot*, but when Riley started *Red Riding Hood*, the soggy shot under Starla's blanket, quivering.

"Who can blame him?" Horatio frowned. "Silly story!"

When the book had been read from cover to cover (and some stories read again!), poor Riley, Horatio and Starla could hardly keep their eyes open.

"Time to sleep, then. . ." Starla yawned.

"At last," said Horatio and Riley. Now they wouldn't have cared if an army of raindrops were stomping on the tent in big boots. They were *so* exhausted, they would sleep through *anything*. . .

They wriggled down in their sleeping bags and Horatio tossed Fluffy to the soggy. "Here, cuddle this," he yawned. "Night night."

The soggy blinked, then peered at the teddy, as if he'd never seen one before. "Don't worry," said Riley quickly. "Nice teddy!"

He popped Fluffy under the blanket

with the soggy and settled them down together. "See you in the morning, then!" said Riley, patting the soggy's damp head. But the soggy still looked wide awake. He kept tapping their sleeping bags and nuzzling their feet.

"What *now*?" groaned Horatio.

"Beats me," Riley sighed.

"Maybe a lullaby will help?" suggested Starla.

She patted the soggy. "There, there," she cooed. "I know a lullaby you'll really love and it'll make you *very* sleepy." She gave a huge yawn and the soggy yawned too.

"Right, then," said Starla, and she sang very softly. . .

Twinkle, twinkle, little star!
How I wonder what you are.
Up above the world so high.
Like a diamond in the sky. . .

Slowly, the soggy's eyes started to close and by the time Starla had finished, Riley, Horatio and the soggy were all fast asleep and snoring.

"Ahh," breathed Starla, closing her own eyes too. "*At last. . .*"

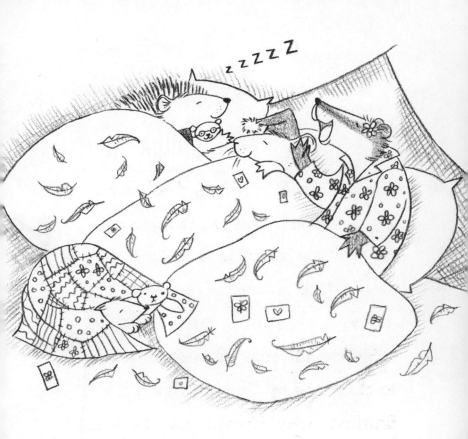

zzzzz

Chapter 6

The next morning, as the sky turned from inky blue to peach and the sun peeped over the hills, everyone in the wonky tent was still fast asleep, even the little soggy.

They would probably have slept on all morning too had a twig outside not suddenly gone *snap*!

"Ahh!" squeaked Riley, sitting up so quickly his nightcap tumbled off. Horatio and Starla sat up too.

"What was *that?*" Horatio yawned.

"I'm not sure," whispered Starla.
Then suddenly, she noticed the soggy.
"Oh dear!" Starla cried, "*Look!*"

Riley and Horatio both looked down.
The soggy, now dry and fluffy, was a ball
of orange fur. His tail had a white tip on
the end and his little ears were pointy.

The soggy was not a
soggy at all. The
soggy was really
. . . *a fox cub!*

Everyone in Willow Valley knew how dangerous foxes can be.

"Don't panic!" cried Riley, quickly. "He won't hurt us! He's just a baby!"

"But what if that snapping noise just now was *Mummy Fox*?" Starla gasped. "What if, now that the rain has stopped, she's sniffed out her little baby?"

"She'll think we've stolen him and she'll have us for breakfast!" wailed Horatio.

No sooner had he said these words but a long, pointy snout poked through the tent door. "Mama!" squealed the baby fox cub. *"Mama!"*

The big mummy fox bounded in and

scooped up her little cub. "My baby!
Oh you're safe!" she breathed, kissing
his head as the others sat very still,
hardly daring to move.

"Mama!" squealed the tiny fox again.

The big mummy fox looked her baby
up and down, making sure he wasn't
hurt. Then she turned to Riley,
Starla and Horatio.

"Thank you," she said to everyone. "You kept my baby safe from the storm."

"Bye bye!" waved the tiny fox cub, beaming.

He wrapped his paws around his mother's neck and she padded across to the door. Then, with a flick of her thick orange tail, they were gone.

Riley, Starla and even Horatio were very quiet now. It had been *quite* a night!

"What shall we do now?" asked Horatio.

"I'm not really sure," muttered Starla.

"Let's go into my house," said Riley. "We can all have breakfast in there."

"Breakfast!" cried Horatio, his prickles

pinging up. "Good idea!"

Riley wandered out of the tent and the others trailed behind. The grass smelled fresh after all that rain, and the patch of toadstools by the blackberry bush looked softer and squashier than ever!

As they walked to the house, birds sang in the trees and the sun shone down on Willow Valley. Flowers were opening, the air was getting warm and a few bright butterflies fluttered by, searching out breakfast in the honeysuckle.

"I'm tired," yawned Riley, rubbing his eyes.

"I am too. . ." muttered Starla.

"But at least we didn't get eaten!" chuckled Horatio.

Back inside, Riley's cave-house was quiet. They tiptoed into the kitchen and sat around the big pine table. "Right then, what's for breakfast?" said Horatio.

With that, Riley's mum came bustling in. "My!" she cried. "You're all up early! Did you sleep well?"

"Yes, thanks, Mum," said Riley as he stifled a yawn. He smiled at his friends as they did the same.

At that moment, Mimi-Rose skipped in. "Riley!" she squeaked. "I made you a present!" And she handed him a painting she'd only just finished upstairs.

"It's you in your tent!" beamed Mimi-Rose, prodding a scruffy brown splatter. "And there is Starla . . . and there is Horatio . . . and there is the moon and the stars!"

Riley looked at the painting and gave
a small grin. There was someone missing.
Someone soggy and small.

"Shall I make us all porridge, then?"
said Riley's mum.

"Oh yes, please!" everyone cried.

"Porridge is *actually* my favourite thing –
except for maybe ginger biscuits . . . Oh,
and ginger cake!" beamed Horatio.

As Riley's mum lit the big black stove,
Riley and his two best friends climbed
into the rocking chair. Camping had
been *quite* an adventure and Riley felt
sure he would do it again. But, right
now, it felt good to be sitting in his

favourite place, warming his toes while his mum cooked a lovely breakfast.

Soon, the dreamy smell of porridge wafted through the air. Mimi-Rose clambered up on to her chair and grabbed her spoon excitedly. "But Mummy – *look!*" she giggled. "Look at Riley!"

Riley's mum was at the dresser gathering mugs and bowls. She turned around. "*Ahh. . .*" she said with a smile.

Riley, Starla *and* Horatio were all fast asleep in the rocking chair, they looked so cosy all huddled up together.

Riley's mum tiptoed over and covered them with her shawl. "Sleep tight," she whispered to the brave little campers.

"Sweet dreams. . ."

Have you read Riley,
Starla and Horatio's
first adventure?

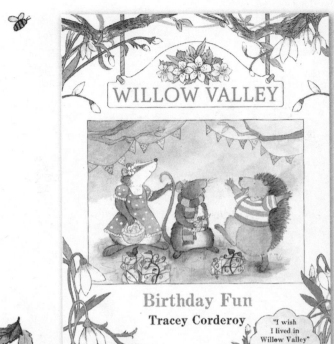

WILLOW VALLEY

Birthday Fun

Tracey Corderoy

"I wish I lived in Willow Valley"
Philippa Forrester

It's Riley's birthday. He can't
wait for his party and to see what
presents his friends have got for him!

Chapter 1

Riley woke from a deep sleep with a big, fluffy wriggle. "Ahhhh. . ." yawned the scruffy little mouse, snuffling into his pillow.

He rubbed his eyes to clear the sleepy dust that had glued them shut. Then he rolled over and gazed at the ceiling.

Slowly a smile spread across Riley's face, stretching from whisker to whisker, as he suddenly remembered what day it was. Today was his *birthday*. At last!

Riley sat up and his tiny pink nose
sniff, sniff, sniffed the air. All was quiet.
He must be the first one awake.

Ribbons of shimmering light crept through the thick stone window, casting bright streaks on to his bedroom walls. It was going to be a clear spring day.

C-r-r-e-e-a-k. Riley's heavy bedroom door opened and a short, plump mouse carrying lots of presents shuffled in.

Riley's mum had twinkly eyes and her coat was thick and shiny. She was chocolate brown, much darker than Riley, whose fur was the colour of toffee. "Happy birthday!" she called brightly.

"Oooh!" gasped Riley. *"Presents!"*

He wriggled out of his thick wool blankets and knelt up on the bed. This

was going to be the best birthday ever!
Later on, he was having a party on the
Whirligig – the biggest of the Willow
Valley narrowboats.

Riley could just imagine it, all done
up with rows of colourful bunting.

There would be presents and games and a birthday cake dotted with flickering candles! He and his friends were going to have so much fun.

As his mum laid Riley's presents on his bed, a tiny white mouse scampered into the room. She was wearing a sparkly tiara and clutching a small, bent wand. "*Riley, wait!*" squeaked his sister, Mimi-Rose. "*I* want to see your presents!"

She clambered up Riley's blankets and plonked herself down beside her big brother. "*Oooh!*" she cried excitedly. "I *wish* it was *my* birthday!"

Riley gazed down at his presents.

They'd been beautifully wrapped in big, shiny leaves and tied with trails of ivy. Some had bunches of fir cones sitting neatly on the top, whilst others had clusters of bright red berries.

Bursting with excitement, Riley picked one up and pulled off its ivy ribbon. The big rhubarb leaf fell open and he lifted out the present inside.

It was a long stripey scarf that his mum had made herself. They'd collected the wool off the hedgerows last summer. Then she'd spun it, and dyed it with autumn berries in shades of blues and purples. She'd knitted it on cold winter nights when Riley and Mimi-Rose had been tucked up in bed.

"Thanks!" said Riley, putting it on. This scarf would come in useful. Even though spring had just arrived, icy winds still whipped through the valley.

"What else have you got?" squeaked Mimi-Rose.

"Let's see!" said Riley. And one by one, he opened his other presents. . .

His sister had painted him a picture, though he wasn't quite sure of what!

"*You!*" she cried, prodding a splodge that looked like a hairy raindrop. "And that's me in my tiara!"

"Of course," grinned Riley. "Err, *thanks*!"

Grandpa's gift was a wooden train set with signals, flags and a driver. "He spent hours making it!" Riley's mum smiled.

Riley also got a spinning top, a shiny bell for his bike and a jam jar filled with berries, seeds and rings of sweet, dried apple.

Now there was only one present left to open. Riley felt along the leafy wrapping. Whatever was in there was long and thin. *"Long and thin!"* he murmured. Maybe – no – it couldn't be! But it *did* feel just the right shape. . .

Riley tore off the leaves. *"It is!"* he cried, and his eyes widened to take in a metal detector! He picked it up. "And look!" he gasped, spotting even more goodies.

There was a pair of binoculars, a little ball of string, a compass, a hat, a small silver spade, a flask, and a notebook and pencil.

"Wow!" cried Riley, leaping off the bed. "A real explorer's kit! Can I go out in the fields and try it? *Please?"*

Riley had wanted to be an explorer for as long as he could remember, just like his dad, Barty Black-Paw, had once been.

"Not so fast!" chuckled his mum.
"You haven't had breakfast yet!
And remember, Riley, when you go
exploring—"

"I know!" Riley replied. "I won't go
into The Dark Wood, I promise!"

His mother nodded and the little
mouse suddenly fell silent. He knew
how dangerous The Dark Wood was.
There had been stories of trees so thick
that they blocked out the sun and no
flowers could grow. So that daytime
looked as gloomy as night. So that
anyone – even the *best* explorers – could

get lost . . . for ever.

Riley had often asked about the night his dad had gone exploring in The Dark Wood. The fog had been thick. The moon milky white. And Barty Black-Paw had never returned. . .

Look out for more

titles — out now!

WILLOW VALLEY

The Big Bike Race

Tracey Corderoy

"I wish I lived in Willow Valley!" **Philippa Forrester**

The school bully has entered
Riley in a bike race, even though he
knows Riley can't ride very well. Can
Riley's friends help him learn in time?

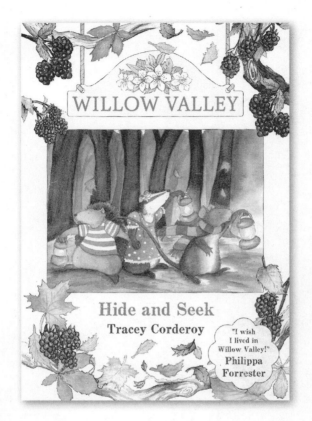

WILLOW VALLEY

Hide and Seek
Tracey Corderoy

"I wish
I lived in
Willow Valley!"
Philippa
Forrester

Riley's little sister, Mimi-Rose, can
be very annoying. But when no one can
find her after a game of hide-and-seek,
Riley hopes she hasn't got lost!